Blippo & Beep

For Lulu and Charlie,
with love from Gigi—SW
For my principal, Mrs. Davis—JE

PENGUIN WORKSHOP
An imprint of Penguin Random House LLC, New York

First published simultaneously in paperback and hardcover in the United States of America by Penguin Workshop, an imprint of Penguin Random House LLC, New York, 2022

Text copyright © 2022 by Sarah Weeks
Illustrations copyright © 2022 by Joey Ellis

Visit us online at penguinrandomhouse.com.

Library of Congress Cataloging-in-Publication Data is available.

Manufactured in China

ISBN 9780593226964 (pbk)

10 9 8 7 6 5 4 3 2 1 TOPL

by Sarah Weeks
illustrated by Joey Ellis

Penguin Workshop

CHAPTER ONE

Beep Tells a Joke

Hey, Blippo, do you want to hear a joke?

Yes, please!

5

6

7

11

Do you want to hear a joke, Beep?

Is it a knock-knock joke?

19

21

23

25

26

27

Because **THIS** time, it made you laugh!

TICKLE

TICKLE

TICKLE

Blippo Tells a New Joke

37

43

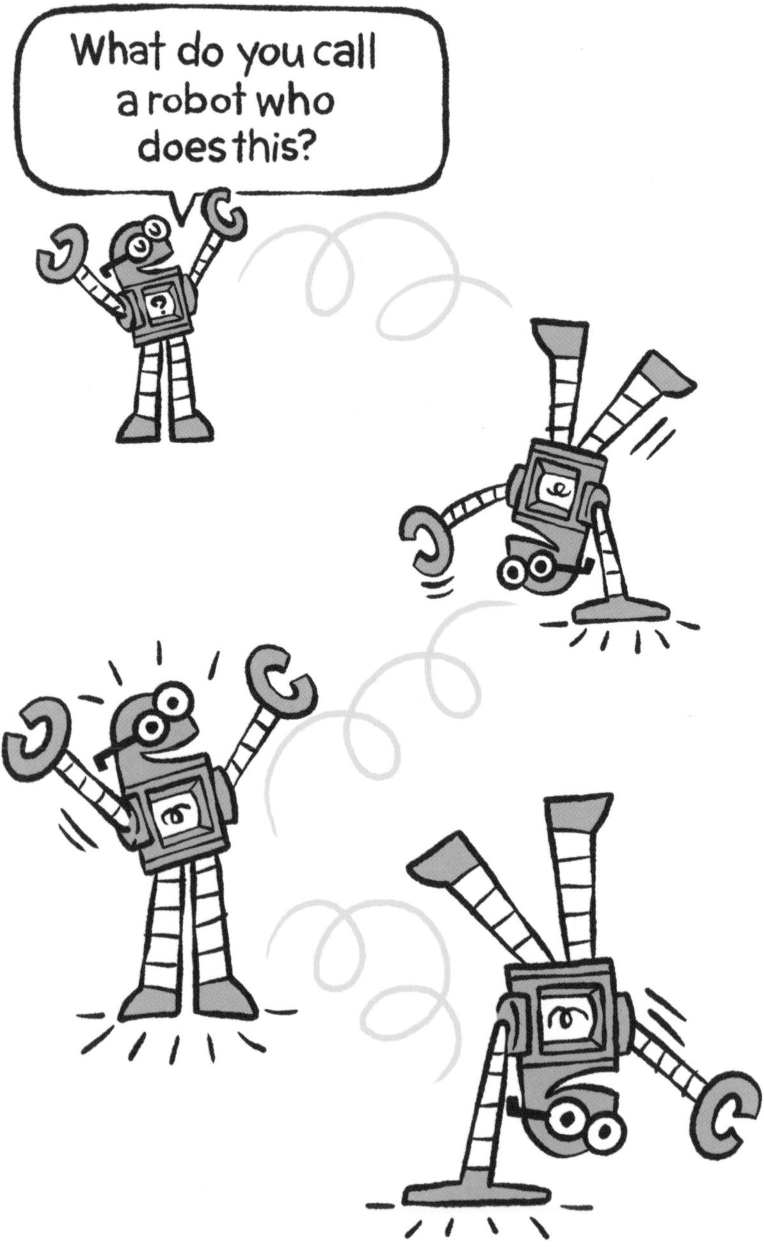
What do you call
a robot who
does this?

45

47